BIMBISARA

BHATTIYA, THE RULER OF MAGADHA, WAS RETURNING TO HIS CAPITAL AT RAJAGRIHA AFTER A BATTLE WITH BRAHMADATTA, THE KING OF ANGA.
BIMBISARA, HIS YOUNGEST SON, RAN OUT TO MEET HIM.
FATHER! YOU'RE BACK...
YES. BUT WE LOST THE BATTLE, MY SON.
OH!
ONE DAY I'LL TEACH THAT TYRANT A LESSON HE'LL NEVER FORGET.

THE NEXT MORNING BHATTIYA STARED THOUGHTFULLY INTO THE MIRROR.
ANOTHER GRAY HAIR!
IT'S TIME TO THINK OF MY SUCCESSOR!
SO SOON, MY LORD!
YES, MY QUEEN. IT WOULD BE FOLLY NOT TO DO SO.
WHO DO YOU THINK SHOULD BE THE CROWN PRINCE?
ISN'T IT THE BIRTHRIGHT OF THE ELDEST? OR IS THERE A CHOICE?
WELL, IF THERE IS?
THEN THE BRAVEST AND THE MOST INTELLIGENT SHOULD BE CHOSEN.
AND SO HE SHALL!

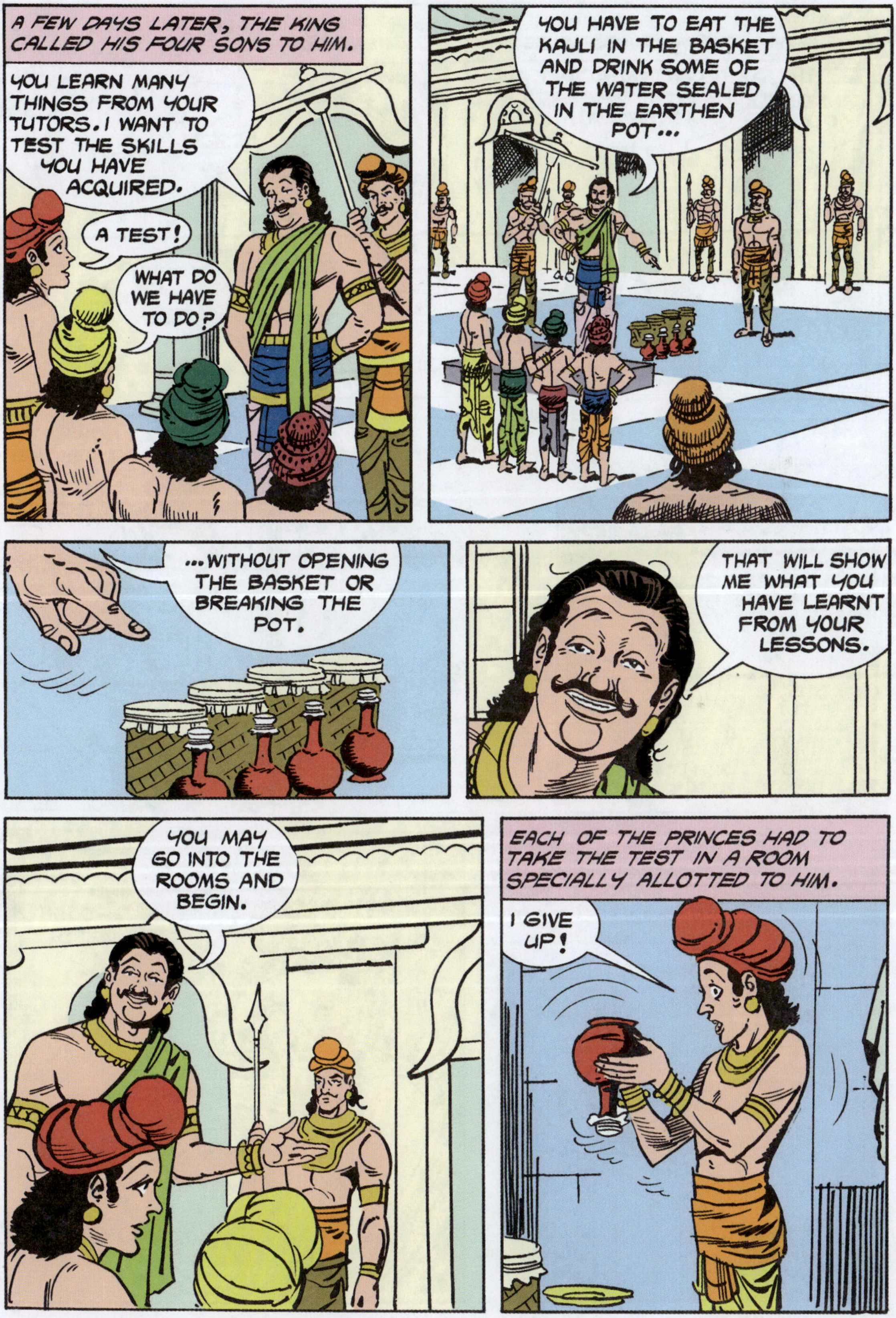
A FEW DAYS LATER, THE KING CALLED HIS FOUR SONS TO HIM.
YOU LEARN MANY THINGS FROM YOUR TUTORS. I WANT TO TEST THE SKILLS YOU HAVE ACQUIRED.
A TEST!
WHAT DO WE HAVE TO DO?
YOU HAVE TO EAT THE KAJLI IN THE BASKET AND DRINK SOME OF THE WATER SEALED IN THE EARTHEN POT...
...WITHOUT OPENING THE BASKET OR BREAKING THE POT.
THAT WILL SHOW ME WHAT YOU HAVE LEARNT FROM YOUR LESSONS.
YOU MAY GO INTO THE ROOMS AND BEGIN.
EACH OF THE PRINCES HAD TO TAKE THE TEST IN A ROOM SPECIALLY ALLOTTED TO HIM.
I GIVE UP!

AS THE ELDEST PRINCE CAME OUT, THE SECOND AND THE THIRD WERE ALREADY THERE.
IT CANNOT BE DONE!
IT CERTAINLY CAN'T. AND I'M SURE BIMBISARA WILL AGREE WITH US.
WHAT KEEPS HIM SO LONG?
INSIDE THE ROOM ALLOTTED TO BIMBISARA—
IF YOU CAN'T GET OVER AN OBSTACLE GO THROUGH IT. HM-M-M...
NOW TO TACKLE THE KAJLI... ON THE SAME PRINCIPLE.
IF... IF I SHAKE THE BASKET VIGOROUSLY ENOUGH, THE KAJLI SHOULD CRUMBLE...
...AND SLIP THROUGH THE GAPS.

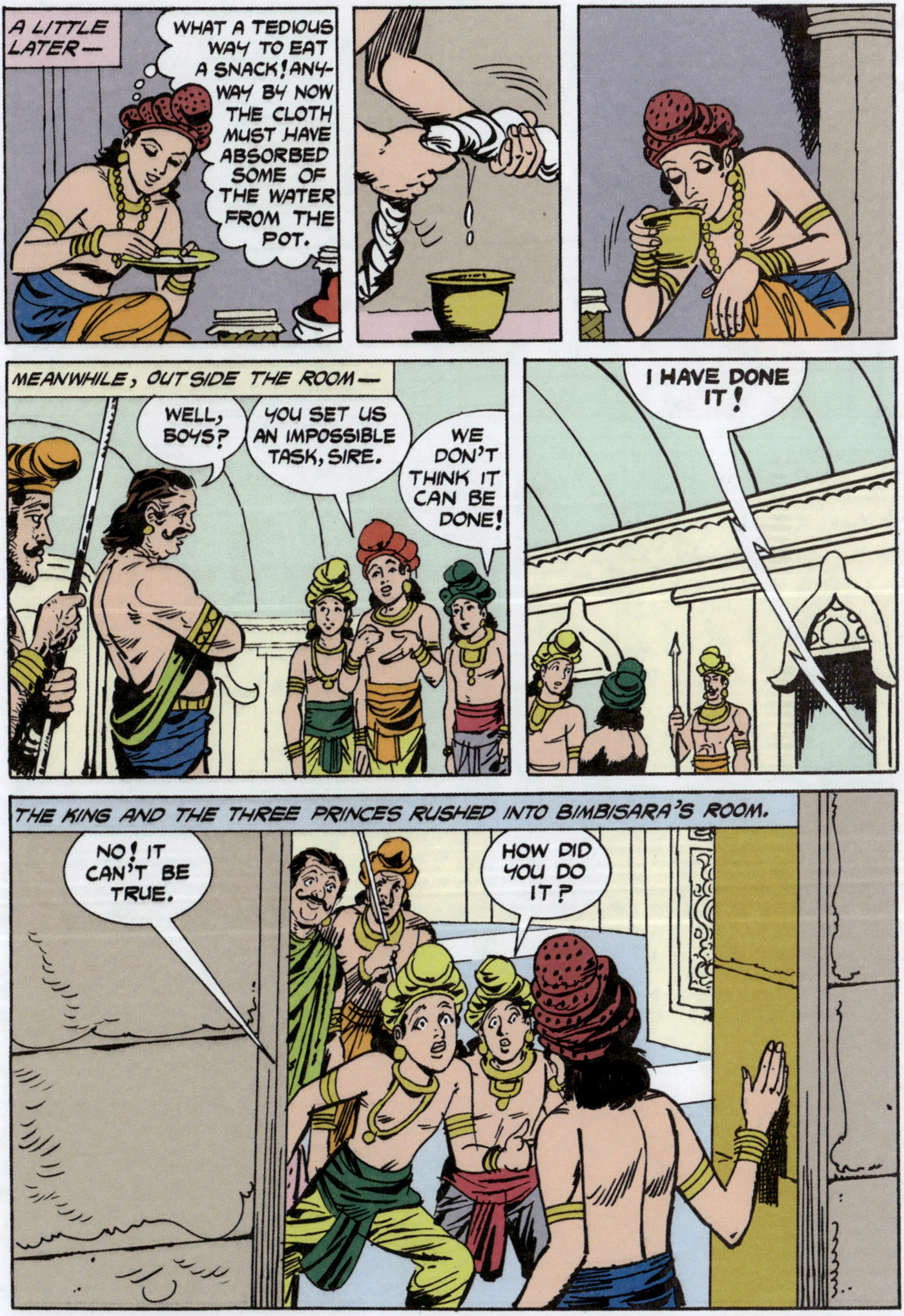
A LITTLE LATER—
WHAT A TEDIOUS WAY TO EAT A SNACK! ANYWAY BY NOW THE CLOTH MUST HAVE ABSORBED SOME OF THE WATER FROM THE POT.
MEANWHILE, OUTSIDE THE ROOM—
WELL, BOYS?
YOU SET US AN IMPOSSIBLE TASK, SIRE.
WE DON'T THINK IT CAN BE DONE!
I HAVE DONE IT!
THE KING AND THE THREE PRINCES RUSHED INTO BIMBISARA'S ROOM.
NO! IT CAN'T BE TRUE.
HOW DID YOU DO IT?

SIMPLE! DON'T YOU REMEMBER THE LESSON ON TACKLING OBSTACLES?
YES. BUT THAT WAS ONLY FOR GETTING THROUGH FORTS.
NOT EARTHEN POTS!
NOR BASKETS!
BIMBISARA, I'M GLAD YOU USED YOUR INTELLIGENCE!
GO NOW, ALL OF YOU, YOUR DINNER IS WAITING. YOU MUST BE HUNGRY!
A GRAND FEAST WAS SPREAD OUT IN THE DINING HALL. AS THE PRINCES ENTERED, THEY DID NOT KNOW THAT THIS WAS YET ANOTHER TEST — OF THEIR COURAGE THIS TIME.

JUST WHEN THEY WERE ABOUT TO BEGIN—
WOOF!
WOOF!
STAY STILL. DON'T MOVE.
DISCRETION IS THE BETTER PART OF VALOUR. LET'S FLEE.
AND THEY FLED. AS THE DOGS WERE ABOUT TO POUNCE ON BIMBISARA...
...HE CALMLY HELD OUT A BOWL OF FOOD.
THE HUNGRY DOGS SETTLED DOWN TO EAT WHILE BIMBISARA WENT ON WITH HIS MEAL.

THE VERY NEXT DAY THE KING CALLED AN ASSEMBLY OF HIS MINISTERS AND PROMINENT CITIZENS.
THOUGH THE YOUNGEST, BIMBISARA HAS PROVED TO BE THE BEST. I APPOINT HIM MY SUCCESSOR.
SOON BIMBISARA WAS ANOINTED AS THE CROWN PRINCE.
OUR BLESSINGS GO WITH YOU, SON!
RISE, MY SON, I AM HAPPY, INDEED.
BIMBISARA, WHAT WOULD YOU LIKE TO DO MOST WHEN YOU BECOME THE KING?
TO CONQUER ANGA AND SUBDUE BRAHMADATTA.
DON'T BE IN A HURRY, SON! BRAHMADATTA IS STRONG AND YOU SHOULD BIDE YOUR TIME.
I WILL MAKE A MOVE ONLY WHEN I AM FULLY PREPARED.

BEFORE LONG, THE KING PASSED AWAY AND BIMBISARA, WHO WAS BARELY FIFTEEN, ASCENDED THE THRONE.
THOUGH YOUNG IN YEARS, BIMBISARA HAD ALREADY FORMED A CLEAR PLAN TO EXPAND THE MAGADHAN EMPIRE.
THE FIRST TO BE CONQUERED NATURALLY WERE THE STATES IN THE NEIGHBOURHOOD.
THERE WERE ALSO SKIRMISHES WITH THE POWERFUL LICHCHHAVIS.
AT VAISHALI, THE LEADERS OF THE LICHCHHAVI REPUBLICS MET UNDER THE CHIEF, RAJA CHETAKA.
BIMBISARA THREATENS WAR! BUT I DO NOT WANT THE KING OF MAGADHA FOR AN ENEMY.
WE TRUST YOUR JUDGEMENT, CHETAKA.

*ONE WHOSE ENEMY IS NOT BORN-HENCE, ONE WHO IS EVER VICTORIOUS.

AS THE DAY OF THE BIRTH OF THE ROYAL CHILD DREW NEAR, BIMBISARA HAD TO LEAVE ON A TOUR OF THE PROVINCES.
I COME TO TAKE LEAVE OF YOU, MY QUEEN. WHEN I RETURN, MY PRINCE IN YOUR ARMS WILL WELCOME ME!
MY AJATASHATRU! HOW FOND HAVE I GROWN OF HIM ALREADY! TAKE CARE OF YOURSELF, MY QUEEN.
I WILL, MY LORD.
A FEW DAYS LATER, BIMBISARA WAS ON HIS WAY BACK TO HIS CAPITAL.
MY SON MUST HAVE COME INTO THE WORLD. I MUST HURRY HOME.
SUDDENLY—
WA...A, WA...A.
IT'S A NEWBORN, SIR. HE SEEMS TO BE OF NOBLE PARENTAGE.

THE POOR THING IS BLEEDING! WHO COULD HAVE ABANDONED SUCH A SWEET BABY?
WHY DO I FEEL SO POWERFULLY DRAWN TOWARDS HIM? DOES EVERY NEW FATHER FEEL LIKE THIS WHEN HE LOOKS AT ANY CHILD?
TAKE GOOD CARE OF HIM. HE SHALL BE A PLAYMATE TO MY PRINCE! LET US HURRY HOME.
AS SOON AS HE REACHED THE PALACE, BIMBISARA RUSHED TO THE QUEEN'S APARTMENTS.
HE'S COME!
WHERE IS MY PRINCE?
HE... HE IS SLEEPING... MY LORD!
THEN LET HIM NOT BE DISTURBED. I WILL GO TO HIM.
NO! NO! MY LORD! YOU MUST NOT LEAVE MY SIDE.

GO SUKESHA! BRING THE PRINCE HERE.
YES... MY LORD.
OH, GOD! WHAT SHALL I DO?
SOMETHING SEEMS TO BE BOTHERING THE MAID...
THE NEXT MOMENT—
THE PRINCE! THE PRINCE IS NOT IN HIS CRADLE!
NO!
SUKESHA RUSHED OUT OF THE NURSERY.
THE PRINCE HAS DISAPPEARED!
GO, LOOK AGAIN!
NO, YOU DON'T HAVE TO LOOK FOR HIM.
CHELLANA, YOU KNEW THAT THE PRINCE WAS NOT IN THERE, DIDN'T YOU?

LOOK INTO MY EYES AND ANSWER ME, CHELLANA.
FORGIVE ME, MY LORD. IT'S TRUE I ABANDONED OUR SON BUT I DID IT TO SAVE YOUR LIFE.
TO SAVE MY LIFE ?
YES, MY LORD. I HAD TO MAKE A CHOICE.
EVER SINCE THE DAY I WAS WITH CHILD, A STRANGE ANXIETY AND RESTLESSNESS HAD GRIPPED ME.
I DID NOT SPEAK OF IT — NOT EVEN TO YOU — HOPING THAT THE MALADY WOULD PASS.
BUT IT ONLY GREW WORSE. SO TAKING ADVANTAGE OF YOUR ABSENCE I CONSULTED THE SOOTHSAYER.

HE DIVINED THAT THE CHILD WHOM I CARRIED MIGHT ONE DAY TAKE YOUR LIFE!
CHELLANA, MY POOR CHELLANA.
I WOULD GIVE UP MY LIFE A HUNDRED TIMES TO BE ABLE TO FONDLE MY CHILD JUST ONCE.
WHAT HAVE I DONE! OH! WHAT HAVE I DONE!
DON'T GRIEVE, CHELLANA. THE CHILD I FOUND BY THE WAYSIDE WILL TAKE THE PLACE OF THE ONE WE LOST!
YOU FOUND AN INFANT? ON THE WAYSIDE? WHERE IS HE?

THEN BIMBISARA ORDERED THAT THE CHILD HE HAD FOUND IN THE FOREST BE BROUGHT IN.
THIS— THIS IS OUR SON! I KNOW. LOOK, MY ROBE! THE ONE I WRAPPED HIM IN!
MY CHILD! THANK GOD YOU ARE ALIVE!
LOOK AT HIM! SEE HOW HE SMILES IN HIS SLEEP!
NO HARM SHOULD EVER COME TO HIM AND HE SHOULD NEVER HEAR OF THIS.

YEARS PASSED. THERE WERE ADDITIONS TO THE ROYAL FAMILY. BIMBISARA OFTEN WATCHED THE PRINCES AT PLAY.
COME ! WE SHALL STORM AND CAPTURE THE ENEMY FORT IN THOSE HILLS. MARCH!
HERE WE COME !
AJATASHATRU IS DESTINED TO BE A GREAT WARRIOR ONE DAY ! SEE HOW HE WIELDS HIS SWORD !
MAY HIS SWORD NEVER BE USED AGAINST YOU, THE KING!
ONE DAY AS BIMBISARA TOOK A ROUND OF THE CITY—
WHO IS THAT ASCETIC? HIS VERY LOOKS SEEM TO SPREAD PEACE AND GOODNESS.
HE IS THE SAKYA PRINCE.
SO THIS IS GAUTAMA, THE PRINCE OF KAPILAVASTU!

BIMBISARA WALKED UP TO THE YOUNG ASCETIC.
WHAT A COMMANDING FACE! HE IS BORN TO RULE!
THESE ROBES OF AN ASCETIC DO NOT BEFIT YOU, GAUTAMA. COME WITH ME, I'LL MAKE YOU THE KING OF HALF OF MAGADHA.
SUCH KINGDOMS ARE NOT FOR ME. I HAVE ALREADY WALKED AWAY FROM ONE!
BUT WHY, O GAUTAMA?
WHAT DO YOU EXPECT TO GAIN BY GIVING UP ALL YOUR POSSESSIONS?
I SEEK THE CAUSE OF THE MISERY WHICH I SEE ALL AROUND...
...AND THE WAY TO END IT.

WHEN YOU LEARN THE WAY TO END MISERY, PRAY COME BACK AND TEACH US.
IF YOU SO WISH.
GAUTAMA WALKED AWAY...
...AND BIMBISARA TURNED TO MATTERS OF STATE. ONE DAY—
REPORTS FROM ANGA ARE DISTURBING, SIR.
BRAHMADATTA HAS ONCE AGAIN BEGUN TO HARASS OUR PEOPLE ON THE BORDERS!
BRAHMADATTA SHOULD BE TAUGHT A LESSON HE WILL NEVER FORGET!
THE VERY WORDS I UTTERED MANY YEARS AGO!
WE SHALL MARCH ON ANGA AND YOU SHALL LEAD THE FORCES.

AJATASHATRU CAREFULLY PLANNED HIS TACTICS AND LED THE FORCES IN THE CAMPAIGN AGAINST ANGA.
HAIL PRINCE AJATASHATRU, THE CONQUEROR OF ANGA.
YOU HAVE PROVED YOURSELF A CLEVER SOLDIER, SON!
IF THIS VICTORY IS BECAUSE OF ME, THE LAND I WON SHOULD BE MINE.
BE MY REGENT HERE, IN ANGA, THEN.
THUS AJATASHATRU REMAINED BEHIND IN ANGA AS THE REGENT.

BIMBISARA SET OUT FOR MAGADHA.
IN THE DAYS TO COME AJATASHATRU WILL MAKE MAGADHA THE GREATEST POWER IN THE LAND!
YET HOW DIFFERENT HE IS FROM THAT SAKYA PRINCE WHO RENOUNCED HIS KINGDOM!
HIS COMPASSIONATE FACE OFTEN COMES TO MY MIND. I LONG TO MEET HIM AGAIN...
A FEW MONTHS LATER —
YOUR MAJESTY, A MONK HAS ARRIVED IN RAJAGRIHA. HE SAYS HE HAS COME TO KEEP AN OLD PROMISE HE MADE.
A MONK?

BIMBISARA IMMEDIATELY WENT TO MEET THE MONK.
GAUTAMA...
...THE BUDDHA! YOU HAVE FOUND THE WAY, AND COME TO TEACH US, THEN!
LATER WHEN BUDDHA LEFT MAGADHA, BIMBISARA WALKED BEHIND HIM UPTO THE BORDER...
...AND SAW HIM OFF.
I AM AS CAPABLE AS MY COUSIN—BUT HE HAS WON THE PATRONAGE OF THE EMPEROR, AND PEOPLE FLOCK TO HIM!
IT WAS DEVADATTA, BUDDHA'S WICKED, AMBITIOUS COUSIN WHO ASPIRED TO BE THE LEADER OF THE MONKS.
I TOO MUST SEEK MY PATRON—AJATASHATRU, THE FUTURE EMPEROR!

WHEN DEVADATTA REACHED THE COURT OF AJATASHATRU, THE PRINCE WAS TRYING A CASE.
VENERABLE MONK, YOU COME AT THE RIGHT TIME.
THE PRINCE NARRATED THE FACTS OF THE CASE TO THE MONK.
YET THE PRISONER SAYS HE IS INNOCENT. DEVADATTA, WHAT DO YOU THINK?
HE LIES! HIS RIGHT HAND SHOULD BE CUT OFF. LET IT BE A LESSON TO OTHERS.
YOU ARE SHREWD IN UNDERSTANDING MEN'S MINDS, DEVADATTA! YOU COULD BE OF GREAT HELP TO ME!
A FEW MONTHS LATER—
I DON'T KNOW WHAT I'D DO WITHOUT YOU, DEVADATTA! YOU ARE SUCH A HELP TO ME!
I COULD BE OF EVEN GREATER HELP.

I WOULD HELP YOU TO THE THRONE OF MAGADHA! YOU CANNOT REMAIN THE GOVERNOR OF A DISTANT PROVINCE FOR EVER!
I AM STILL TOO YOUNG.
BIMBISARA WAS ONLY FIFTEEN WHEN HE CAME TO THE THRONE.
ALL IN GOOD TIME, DEVADATTA.
THE BEST TIME IS— NOW!
HOW LONG WILL YOU WAIT, AJATASHATRU? LIFE IS SHORT. ACT! ACT BEFORE IT IS TOO LATE.
TAKE THE REINS OF THE KINGDOM IN YOUR HANDS— BY FORCE IF NECESSARY.

FORCE ?
FORCE DID YOU SAY ?
WHAT CAN I, A MONK, TEACH YOU ABOUT THE SOLDIER'S CRAFT ?
AND DEVADATTA LEFT, SATISFIED. HE KNEW THAT HIS WORDS HAD FOUND THEIR MARK AT LAST.
A FEW WEEKS LATER WHEN BIMBISARA WAS FAST ASLEEP AT NIGHT—
BRING THE LIGHT.
WHO ARE YOU ? YOU SCOUNDREL !

THE KING WOKE UP AND SAW THE MAN WHO HAD COME TO KILL HIM.
MY SON!
RELEASE THE PRINCE.
SIR, THE PRINCE IS GUILTY OF A HEINOUS CRIME! HE DESERVES THE MOST SEVERE PUNISHMENT!
DID YOU NOT HEAR THE ORDER I GAVE? RELEASE THE PRINCE!
WHAT IS IT YOU WANT, AJATASHATRU?
THE KINGDOM— BEFORE IT IS TOO LATE!
THE KINGDOM IS YOURS. NOW IF YOU WANT IT. THIS DRAMA WAS NOT NECESSARY!

MISTAKING HIS FATHER'S LOVE FOR COWARDICE, AJATASHATRU PROCLAIMED THAT THE EMPEROR WAS AILING AND RULED IN HIS PLACE.
BUT IN FACT BIMBISARA WAS CONFINED TO HIS CHAMBER.
THIS IS INTOLERABLE! I WILL REMIND THE PRINCE OF HIS DUTIES TO HIS ELDERS.
NO, DEAR QUEEN! WISDOM SHOULD DAWN FROM WITHIN.
DEVADATTA CONTINUED TO WIELD HIS INFLUENCE ON AJATASHATRU.
WELCOME, MY FRIEND!
AH! NOW YOU ARE THE RULER. BUT HOW SAFE ARE YOU? ALL THE NOBLES AND SOLDIERS WOULD TURN AGAINST YOU AT A SIGN FROM BIMBISARA!
TO SAFEGUARD HIS POSITION, AJATASHATRU REMOVED BIMBISARA TO A PRISON CELL.
THERE SHOULD BE GUARDS ALL DAY AND NIGHT HERE. NO ONE SHOULD APPROACH THE EMPEROR WITHOUT MY PERMISSION.

WHAT A PERVERSE STATE, MY LORD!
TAKE HEART, MY QUEEN! REMEMBER THE PRINCE WHO SPURNED HIS KINGDOM TO REDEEM MANKIND.
YOU ARE NOW MY EYES AND EARS. TELL ME ALL THE NEWS.
BUT CHELLANA WAS SO OVERCOME BY GRIEF, SHE COULD NOT SPEAK!
SPEAK TO ME, CHELLANA! HOW FARES OUR DAUGHTER-IN-LAW? WHEN WILL YOU BE A GRANDMOTHER? HOW ARE THE OTHER PRINCES?
THEY HAVE FLED TO VAISHALI. THEY DID NOT FEEL SAFE HERE ANY MORE.
I AM NOT SURPRISED, AND AT THE SAME TIME, I FEEL SAD!
I FEEL MORE THAN SAD, MY LORD! I AM ALARMED. THAT PROPHECY...
FEAR NOT CHELLANA. HE IS MY SON! THE HOT-HEADED YOUTH IS MISGUIDED. HE WILL SOON REALISE HIS MISTAKE.

MONTHS PASSED. BIMBISARA CONTINUED TO LANGUISH IN PRISON. AJATASHATRU WAS VIRTUALLY THE RULER.
AJATASHATRU, WHEN WILL I HEAR PEOPLE HAILING YOU AS MAHARAJ?
WELL...
SOON YOU WILL BECOME A FATHER. YOUR CHILD WILL GROW UP TO BE A YOUNG PRINCE. AND YOU WILL STILL BE A PRINCE—THOUGH OLD ENOUGH TO BE A KING!
ISSUE THE ORDER, AJATASHATRU. HAVE THE OLD KING EXECUTED AND RULE IN YOUR OWN RIGHT!
WELL, DEVADATTA. I SHALL BE GUIDED BY YOUR ADVICE.
AJATASHATRU SENT FOR AN OFFICER.
GIVE THESE ORDERS TO THE PRISON WARDEN. I WANT THEM CARRIED OUT IMMEDIATELY.
LATER—
TWO COMMUNICATIONS FOR YOUR MAJESTY!
TAKE THIS, O BEARER OF GLAD TIDINGS! A SON IS BORN TO ME TODAY.

HOW STRONG IS THIS LOVE FOR MY SON COURSING THROUGH MY HEART THOUGH I HAVE YET TO SEE HIM.
SUDDENLY—
THE KING, MY FATHER—HE TOO, MUST HAVE FELT THE SAME WAY WHEN HE FIRST HEARD OF MY COMING?
AND I, HIS SON, HAVE GIVEN ORDERS TO EXECUTE HIM!
NO! MY FATHER SHALL NOT DIE! I WILL REVERSE MY ORDERS.
REALISATION THAT HE WAS BEING MISLED CAME TO AJATASHATRU, BUT A LITTLE TOO LATE. THE SECOND LETTER WAS FROM THE WARDEN OF THE PRISON TO REPORT THAT HIS ORDERS HAD BEEN CARRIED OUT.
OH, NO! I HAVE PUT MY OWN FATHER TO DEATH! FIE ON ME!
JUST THEN—
DEVADATTA WISHES TO SEE YOU, SIRE.
WHAT! THAT WRETCH!
TELL HIM I SHALL NOT SET EYES ON HIM AGAIN AS LONG AS I LIVE.
AJATASHATRU ASCENDED THE THRONE AND WENT ON TO MAKE MAGADHA THE SUPREME POWER AND FULFIL THE DREAMS OF HIS FATHER. IT WAS HOWEVER THE VISION OF BIMBISARA AND THE LOVE HE BORE HIS SON WHICH MADE IT POSSIBLE.

THE ACK QUIZ

BRAVEHEARTS

1 What was the name of Rani Lakshmibai's kingdom?

2 What was the capital of Ashoka's kingdom?

3 She was the only queen to rule from the throne of Delhi. Who was she?

4 Which dynasty did she belong to?

5 Who did she succeed to the throne?

6 Who is the person in the picture?

7 With whom did he climb Mt Everest?

8 In which year did he climb Mt Everest?

9 What was the name of Rana Pratap's horse?

10 Who were the two people hanged along with Bhagat Singh?

ANSWERS

1. Jhansi 2. Pataliputra 3. Razia Sultan 4. Mamluk/Slave dynasty 5. Iltutmish 6. Tenzing Norgay 7. Edmund Hillary 8. 1953 9. Chetak 10. Rajguru and Sukhdev

THE ACK QUIZ

BRAVEHEARTS

1 What is India's highest military award?

2 Name the IAF pilot who won the award in the 1971 conflict?

3 Who is the person in the picture?

4 What was he popularly known as?

5 Who did he succeed as leader of the INA?

6 Who is the person in the picture?

7 Where was she born?

8 She first flew on space shuttle ____________.

9 Rani Chenamma was the queen of which kingdom?

10 Who was the queen who fought against the Mughals in the battle of Ahmednagar?

ANSWERS

1. Param Vir Chakra 2. Flying Officer Nirmaljit Singh Sekhon 3. Subhas Chandra Bose 4. Netaji 5. Rash Behari Bose 6. Kalpana Chawla 7. Karnal, Haryana (erstwhile Punjab) 8. Columbia 9. Kittur 10. Chand Bibi